MICHAEL BOND

PADDINGTON

AT THE CIRCUS

illustrated by R. W. ALLEY

HARPER
An Imprint of HarperCollins*Publishers*

One morning Paddington was doing his shopping in the market when he saw a very tall man with a pointed hat and baggy trousers.

The man was putting up a poster, and he was so tall, he didn't even need a ladder to reach the top of the billboard.

The poster showed a huge tent decorated with colored lights, and across the middle were the words SEE THE WORLD'S GREATEST CIRCUS. ONE NIGHT ONLY.

Paddington rubbed his eyes several times in order to make sure he wasn't dreaming.

Paddington hurried back home to tell the others
what he had seen.

"The world's greatest circus?" repeated Jonathan,
giving his sister a wink. "Are you sure?"

"It's for one night only!" exclaimed Paddington.

"Don't worry," said Judy. "You won't miss it."

"Dad's got tickets for the front row," added Jonathan. "Mrs. Bird's coming, too."

Paddington had never been to a circus before, and he was very excited at the thought. "I hope it gets dark early," he said. "Then we can see the lights."

Paddington's wish came true. Seen from the outside, with all the colored lights twinkling against the night sky, the circus really did have a magical air.

"Hurry! Hurry! Have your tickets ready!" called a voice. "The show's about to begin!"

"It's the man I saw this morning," whispered Paddington. "The very tall one I was telling you about."

"That's one of the clowns," said Judy.

"He isn't really that tall . . . ," began Jonathan. But Paddington couldn't wait. He could hear a band playing, and he was already hurrying on ahead.

But if the outside of the tent had seemed exciting, it was nothing compared to the inside.

There was a lovely smell of sawdust, and in among the jugglers and the acrobats there was even a girl selling ice cream.

Mr. Brown pointed to a man in the middle of the ring. He was wearing a top hat.

"That's the ringmaster," he explained. "He's in charge of everything."

"I expect you could keep a lot of marmalade sandwiches under a hat like that," said Paddington enviously. "I think I would like to be a ringmaster one day."

Just then the tall clown entered the ring. He was clutching a long pole that had a bucket balanced on the end of it. When he saw Paddington waving, he came across to greet him.

"Watch out!" cried Jonathan as the clown leaned over to shake Paddington's paw.

Paddington jumped up in alarm. But he wasn't quick enough. Before he had time to escape, the bucket had fallen off the end of the pole.

Luckily, it was tied on with string and it was empty, so Paddington didn't get wet.

"Clowns are full of tricks," said Judy.

"I'm glad I was wearing my duffle coat all the same," said Paddington. "Someone might have put water in the bucket by mistake."

"I'm told ice cream is very good for young bears if they've had a shock," said Mr. Brown.

He ordered six large cones, then they all sat back to enjoy the show.

"I feel better already, Mr. Brown," said Paddington gratefully.

Paddington had hardly started on his ice cream when he had yet another shock.

Glancing up toward the roof of the tent, he saw a man hanging from a rope.

Jonathan looked at his program. "That must be one of the Popular Prices," he said. "They're trapeze artists."

"Don't worry!" called Paddington. "I'm coming. Bears are good at climbing."

Before the others could stop him, Paddington was halfway up the nearest tent pole.

Climbing the pole and carrying an ice cream at the same time wasn't easy, and the audience gave a round of applause when he reached the safety of a small platform near the top.

Paddington was about to take a bow when, to his surprise, he saw a man coming toward him on a bicycle.

"I don't think you're supposed to bring your bicycle up here, Mr. Price!" he exclaimed.

"Look out!" shouted the man, frantically ringing his bell. "I can't stop!"

"Hold on!" called his partner.

In the confusion, Paddington didn't know which to do first, so he grabbed hold of a nearby bar.

It came away in his paw, and before he knew what was happening, he felt himself flying through the air.

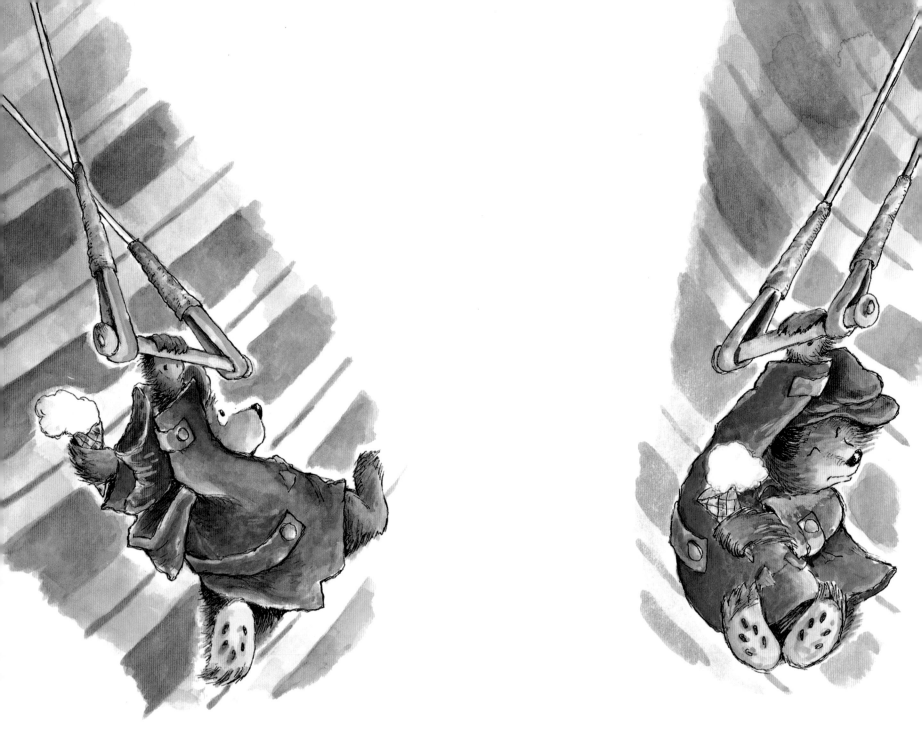

The audience thought Paddington was part of the act, and they clapped louder than ever.

Then a gasp went up as he missed the platform on the other side of the tent and began swinging backward and forward in midair.

"Oh dear!" said Mrs. Brown. "Whatever will he do now?"

"I shouldn't worry," said Mrs. Bird. "Bears usually land on their feet."

But even Mrs. Bird went quiet as Paddington's swings got slower and slower, until finally he ended up hanging over the middle of the ring.

"Don't let go!" shouted the ringmaster. "Whatever you do—don't let go!"

"I'm not going to!" cried Paddington.

He tried to raise his hat, but he was still holding the ice cream cone in his other paw.

A look of horror came over the ringmaster's face as something soft and white landed with a *squelch* on his beautifully clean top hat.

"Help!" cried Paddington. "I've changed my mind. I can't hold on much longer."

Everybody in the audience began making suggestions, but in the end it was the clown who came to the rescue. Balancing his bucket on the end of the pole, he stretched up as high as he could so Paddington could climb into it.

"I hope the string doesn't break," said Mrs. Bird. "That bear had a very large lunch."

"If the clown stretches any more," said Judy, "his trousers will fall down."

Sure enough they did, and the cheers changed to laughter as
Paddington was lowered to safety.

"Funniest act I've seen in years!" shouted a man near the Browns. "More! More!"

Paddington gave the man a hard stare. "I don't think I want to do any more," he announced. "In fact, I don't think I want to go on a trapeze ever again. I shall just sit and watch from now on."

Then he caught sight of the clown's stilts. "It's no wonder you look so tall!" he exclaimed.

Paddington didn't think anything more *could* happen to him, but at the end of the evening the ringmaster presented him with another ice cream and insisted he take part in the Grand Parade.

"After all," he said, "you *were* the star of the show.

"It's a pity we are moving on," he added, turning to the Browns. "It isn't every evening we have a daring young bear on the flying trapeze."

"If you ask me," said Mrs. Bird wisely, "it's a good thing you don't. Otherwise there's no knowing where you would end up."

Later that evening, when the Browns said good night to Paddington, they found him standing on the box seat by his bedroom window. He had a faraway look in his eyes.

"I was taking a last look at the circus before it goes on its way," he explained.

"Do you still want to be a ringmaster one day?" asked Judy.

Paddington climbed into bed and tested his sheets carefully
to make sure he was safely tucked in before answering. Then he
lay back.

"I think perhaps I would sooner be a clown," he said dreamily.
"It must be nice to be so tall. You can always see what's going on
in the world without having to stand on anything."